LULU'S PIANO LESSON

Arlene Alda

Illustrated by

Lisa Desimini

TUNDRA BOOKS

Published in Canada by Tundra Books,
75 Sherbourne Street, Toronto, Ontario M5A 2P9

Published in the United States by Tundra Books of Northern New York,
P.O. Box 1030, Plattsburgh, New York 12901

Library of Congress Control Number: 2009938087

Library and Archives Canada Cataloguing in Publication

Alda, Arlene, 1933-
      Lulu's piano lesson / Arlene Alda ; illustrated by Lisa Desimini.

For ages 4-7.
ISBN 978-0-88776-930-6

      I. Desimini, Lisa   II. Title.

PZ7.A358Lu 2010   j813'.54   C2009-905773-5

We acknowledge the financial support of the Government of Canada through the Book Publishing Industry Development Program (BPIDP) and that of the Government of Ontario through the Ontario Media Development Corporation's Ontario Book Initiative.
We further acknowledge the support of the Canada Council for the Arts and the Ontario Arts Council for our publishing program.

ONTARIO ARTS COUNCIL
CONSEIL DES ARTS DE L'ONTARIO

Medium: cut-paper collage and digital

Design: Leah Springate

Printed in China

1 2 3 4 5 6   15 14 13 12 11 10

*For music teachers with imagination
and understanding, wherever you are*

A.A.

For Frances

L.D.

"See you next week, Lulu,"
said Mr. Sharp.

On Monday . . .

"Give me a push," said Lulu's sister, Cara. Lulu pushed Cara's swing as high as she could. *Squeak, squeak.* The swing went higher and higher. *Squeak, squeak.* The swing went from up to down.

Lulu got on her own swing and pumped her legs. Closing her eyes, she almost fell asleep to the lullaby of squeaks.

"It's time for your piano practice," called out Mom. Lulu opened her eyes. "Time to practice 'Old MacDonald.'"

"I'm still swinging. Later, please," said Lulu.

"Later" came and "later" went, as Lulu and Cara played in their yard.

On Tuesday . . .

Rrrrring, rrrrring. Lulu pressed the bell on her bike as she and her best friend, Marcie, rode around the corner. *Rrrrring, rrrrring*, as they warned the squirrels to get out of the way. Lulu felt the breeze blowing her hair back from her face. She sang, "Better watch out. Here we come, *ring-a-ring-a-ring!*"

Lulu passed her front door just as Mom called out, "Time to practice the piano. It's nearly dinnertime."

"Soon . . . soon," called out Lulu, as she and Marcie whizzed by once again.

"Soon" came and "soon" went, as Lulu happily rode her bike with Marcie.

On Wednesday . . .

Lulu climbed up to the first branch of the apple tree in her yard. *Thump, thump.* Some apples fell to the ground.

Lulu saw Mom and Cara through the kitchen window. *Hi*, she waved.

Lulu climbed higher just as Mom called out, "Lulu, how about a little piano playing?" *Thump, splat* went some more apples as they fell to the ground and stayed right where they landed.

"I'm still climbing," said Lulu. "Not now."

"Not now" came and "not now" went, as Lulu happily climbed up the tree and jumped down, over and over.

On Thursday . . .

The wind howled *whooo* as the rain poured on the apple tree, poured on the swings, and poured on the street outside the house. Lulu and Cara played inside with their teddy bears.

"It's a great day to practice 'Old MacDonald,'" said Mom.

"In ten minutes," said Lulu.

"Ten minutes" came and "ten minutes" went, as Lulu and Cara switched from teddy bears to stuffed dogs and cats.

And then Friday afternoon arrived . . .
"Time for your piano lesson," said Mom.

Lulu looked surprised. "Today?" she asked. "I really don't want to take my lesson today. . . . I didn't practice."

But Lulu packed up her music and slowly walked to her piano teacher's house. As Lulu walked, the tune of "Old MacDonald" swirled around in her head to the sounds of her own shoes on the sidewalk. *Tip-tap, tip-tap.*

Lulu's stomach felt like it was on a roller coaster, rising and falling with each step she took.

"Hi, Lulu," said her teacher, when he answered the door. "How are you today?"

"Good, Mr. Sharp," said Lulu. Lulu always said "good," even when she didn't really feel that way . . . even when her stomach churned from not having practiced.

Lulu finally blurted out, "I didn't practice this week."

"What fun things did you do instead?" asked Mr. Sharp.

Lulu talked about Cara and Marcie, the swings in her yard, her bike rides, climbing the apple tree, and playing with her stuffed animals. The more she talked, the better she felt.

Lulu forgot all about her stomach ache as she continued. "I'm sorry that I didn't practice the piano this week, but I heard a lot of sounds that were like music to me," she said. "There were *squeaks* from the swings and *thumps* from the apples falling and *rrrrrings* from my bike bell and *whooos* from the wind and *tip-tap, tip-tap* from my shoes to the 'Old MacDonald' song that was playing in my head when I walked here today."

"Can you sing those sounds for me to the tune of 'Old MacDonald'?" Mr. Sharp asked.

"Old MacDonald had a farm, E-I-E-I-O," sang Lulu.
"On his farm he heard his shoes, E-I-E-I-O . . . with
a *tip-tap* here and a *tip-tap* there, here a *tip*, there a *tap*,
everywhere a *tip-tap*."

Lulu liked to sing. It wasn't hard, like reading notes
and playing the piano. She sang on about the sounds of
wind howling, apples falling, swings squeaking, and
bicycle bells ringing.

"Now that you've warmed up, how about playing your lesson at the piano?" asked Mr. Sharp.

"But that's what I didn't practice!" said Lulu.

"Try," said Mr. Sharp.

Lulu stared at the music on the page. At first, the notes looked mostly like black dots on lines. Slowly Lulu figured out what the notes were. She remembered their alphabet names and where they were on the piano keys.

Mr. Sharp helped her whenever she asked.

The song started to come from the piano as Lulu played the notes written on the page. She played them over and over, each time getting more sure of herself . . . each time playing the piece a little faster.

"I did it," she said. "I can read the notes and play the piano at the same time. And I didn't do it later – I did it *now*!" said Lulu proudly.

"And you made up new words to the song, too," added Mr. Sharp.

Lulu felt good. Her teacher clapped his hands loudly. "Bravo, Lulu!" he said. "For next week's lesson, practice 'Old MacDonald' and see if you can memorize the piano part."

Lulu's lesson was over. Her stomach ache was completely gone.

Lulu skipped, Lulu ran, Lulu danced, and Lulu sang all the way home.

The music of the piano lesson was still in Lulu's head, this time played by a huge orchestra . . . where the violins went *squeak, squeak,* the triangle went *rrrrring,* the flutes went *whooo,* the large tympani drum went *thump, thump,* and a *tip-tap, tip-tap* was made by the conductor as her baton kept the beat.

The music of the piano lesson was still in Lulu's head, this time played by a huge orchestra . . . where the violins went *squeak, squeak*, the triangle went *rrrrring*, the flutes went *whooo*, the large tympani drum went *thump, thump*, and a *tip-tap, tip-tap* was made by the conductor as her baton kept the beat.

Of course, Lulu herself was singing along while reading
the notes and playing the piano at the same time.